Book 2
**stop take
walk**

By Tammi Salzano
Illustrated by Duendes del Sur

ISBN 978-0-545-35534-6

12 11 10 9 8 7 6 5 4 3 2 1   11 12 13 14 15/0
                                                        95
Printed in China
First printing, October 2011

SCHOLASTIC INC.
New York   Toronto   London   Auckland
Sydney   Mexico City   New Delhi   Hong Kong

Scooby-Doo and his friends **take** a **walk** to the carnival.
Scooby and Shaggy **stop** to play a game.

The gang **takes** a **walk** to the tent.
They **stop** when they see tracks.
The magic hat is missing.
Did it **take** a **walk**?

Scooby and Shaggy **take** a **walk** to find the hat. They **stop** for a snack. The hat is not there.

Scooby **takes** a **walk** to the balloons.
Stop, Scooby!
The hat is not up there!

Fred, Daphne, and Velma **take** a **walk** to find the hat.
They **stop** at the games.
The hat is not there.

Scooby **takes**
another **walk**.
Where is the hat?
Where will he **stop**?

Stop!
The hat did not **take**
a **walk**.
The clown has the hat.

Scooby-Dooby-Doo!
The gang found the hat!